The Secret Soldier

by Diana Star Helmer

Perfection Learning®

Cover Illustration: Rex Schneider
Inside Illustration: Rex Schneider

Dedication

To Dorothy Francis—for fighting the good fight, and helping us and so many others do the same. Thank you.

About the Author

Diana Star Helmer grew up in Iowa. She loved fireflies, autumn skies, bright snowy nights, and waiting for spring. But she wondered about the ocean, the mountains, and all kinds of art in the city.

She moved near Seattle, Washington, and five happy years later, she suddenly got homesick. So she went home to Iowa with her husband, Thomas S. Owens, who is also an author of children's books. A white cat came to their house one day and never left.

Ms. Helmer loves writing and thinking and drawing and dancing and, of course, Tom and Angel.

Image credits: Art Today pp. 7, 8, 10, 11, 12, 14, 15, 18, 19, 21, 23, 30, 33, 34, 35, 44, 46, 47, 48, 49, 50, 55; Corel p. 39

For information, contact
Perfection Learning® Corporation,
1000 North Second Avenue, P.O. Box 500,
Logan, Iowa 51546-0500.
Phone: 1-800-831-4190 • Fax: 1-712-644-2392
PB ISBN-13: 978-0-7891-5127-8 ISBN-10: 0-7891-5127-8
RLB ISBN-13: 978-0-7807-9281-4 ISBN-10: 0-7807-9281-5
PPI / 10 / 11
11 12 13 14 15 16 PP 16 15 14 13 12 11

Table of Contents

★   ★   ★   ★   ★

Chapter 1

In the Woods

Michael saw them first. They were deeper in the woods. Hidden under a bush were someone's clothes. But whose?

And why was that person hiding in the forest?

"Ssss!" Michael pointed.

Ralph saw it next. "I'll bet it's a spy."

"A spy?" Michael would never have thought of such a thing. But Ralph's idea started Michael thinking a

thousand terrible thoughts. "A spy might follow us to camp. Then bring the British army back to kill us!"

Ralph rolled his eyes. "Our camp is a big training camp. The British already know where it is."

Michael sighed with relief.

"That spy will probably just kill us now," Ralph said.

Michael jumped as Andrew pushed a branch aside to see. "Maybe it's a hurt soldier who needs help," Andrew said.

Michael knew Jacob would be right behind Andrew.

"Maybe it's not a soldier," Jacob whispered. "Maybe it's just a person."

Michael snorted. "We're fighting a

war in these parts! Only soldiers have business in the woods."

"I'll move to where I can see better," Ralph whispered. "When I wave, you shout. He'll show himself. And if his coat is red, we'll shoot him."

Michael nodded and loaded his gun. Ralph always knew what to do.

Michael wasn't always sure about Ralph's ideas. This was one of those ideas. But at least Ralph was doing something.

"No!" Andrew said. "Sometimes our soldiers wear red coats. They take them off dead British soldiers. Our army is short of clothes."

Michael closed his eyes. "When this war is over, maybe the world will make sense again."

Ralph grinned. "War makes a lot of things. But sense isn't one of them. Here I go."

Michael watched Ralph move through the trees. His feet did not make a sound. Ralph aimed his gun at the cloth. He waved.

Michael took a breath. Then he yelled, "HEEYYYYYY!"

The cloth did not move.

"When I say three," Michael whispered to Jacob and Andrew. His heart pounded. "One. Two. THREE!"

The three charged the bush. They roared and waved their guns, knives, and arms.

The cloth still did not move. The boys stopped.

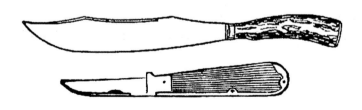

"It's just . . . clothes!" Michael panted. "With nobody in them!"

Andrew bent and held up a woman's long dress. Jacob picked up the petticoats.

"This does not make sense," Michael said. "Who could have left them here?"

"A girl with a bad cold," Ralph grinned.

Andrew and Jacob laughed. Michael didn't.

He was getting an idea.

"I still think it was a spy," Michael said. "A British spy. Dressed as a woman! He could learn our army's secrets. Everyone would trust him."

Chapter **2**

Far from Home

Shadows followed the boys back to camp. Their empty bellies squirmed as they walked.

Michael didn't even notice. He was too proud of his spy idea. Something finally made sense.

Nothing else had made sense since this war started. First, Michael's older brother signed with the Continental Army. Father didn't mind.

Uncle John backed the British. So he and Father had stopped speaking. Visiting the cousins on Sundays had stopped. So did trading garden vegetables for Aunt Lucy's bread and stew.

Aunt Lucy had helped ever since Michael's mother died. That is, she had helped until the war. Then Michael's family had gone hungry.

Then Michael joined the army too. He thought soldiers would get food each day.

But they didn't. In fact, Michael and the others had just been begging for food from farmers.

It doesn't make sense, Michael thought. We are fighting because Britain's King George taxes us. He takes our money. We have nothing. But how can hungry soldiers win a war?

Michael walked alone. Like always.

Ralph marched ten steps ahead. Andrew and Jacob talked together behind Michael. But no one said anything about Michael's idea.

Darkness hid everyone. Michael felt even lonelier.

Finally, the boys trudged into their tent.

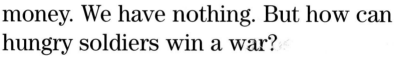

Two boys inside jumped up.

"We're your new messmates," said the tall boy. He held out his hand. "I'm Hugh Sorenson."

The other boy offered his hand too. "Christopher Hunter," he said softly.

Ralph rolled his eyes. "Does your mother know you're here? You don't look old enough to shave."

Christopher blinked. "I know I'm small," he said. "But I thought the army needed men."

Michael held out his hand. "Don't mind Ralph. I'm not 16 yet. I doubt if Ralph is either. But we told the army we were. The army does need you."

"We just don't have much to feed you," Ralph snorted.

"Ralph says that because he burns the food," Andrew said.

"We take turns cooking our rations," Jacob explained. "We don't cook very well."

"But Ralph is the worst," said Andrew. "Poison!"

"Worse than poison," Jacob finished. Michael's brothers sometimes finished Michael's words.

Suddenly, Michael felt homesick. He tried to join in.

"How can something be worse than poison?" he asked.

Jacob blinked. "It's just a saying."

But Hugh laughed.

"No, it's not," he said. "See, poison kills you. But Ralph's cooking doesn't. Which means—"

"—you'll have to eat it again!" Michael laughed. It seemed like the first time Michael had laughed since joining the army.

Ralph liked jokes. He always joked about his cooking. But he wasn't laughing now. His cheeks burned red.

Christopher must have seen Ralph. He didn't laugh either.

But Hugh did. Then he said, "I can cook. I have nine brothers. Someone had to help my mother. I'll cook tonight. You're all tired."

Ralph did not stop glaring.

But he ate more of Hugh's corn pone and beans than anyone else that night.

Chapter 3

War Inside and Out

The British were near. They moved in small groups. They left Tory farms alone. But they robbed and burned the others.

Hugh and Christopher had only been in camp two days when orders came to march. They were to hunt the British robbers. The hunting parties would be big.

18

Groups of 30 men or more.

Michael stayed close to Hugh and Christopher on the march. After all, he had been in the army longer. He could help them. It was better to think about helping than about—

Gunshot spattered ahead.

Michael looked quickly at Hugh.

"Sounds like turkey hunting," Hugh said. "But it isn't."

They ran forward. At the same time, they felt for their bullets and powder. Smoke cut Michael's nose. They reached the clearing.

They were too late. The front marchers had surprised a few redcoats. Michael's captain looked over their bodies. All he saw was red coats and red blood.

"You six!" said the captain, turning to the boys. "Gather the coats and guns. Report back to me with your takings."

There were 12 British bodies. Taking their clothes was not easy. Their arms and legs did not want to move.

The boys worked in pairs. Michael watched Hugh look at the first soldier a long time. He finally knelt by the body. Michael knelt beside him.

"You've seen death before?" Michael asked.

Hugh nodded.

"But not like this?"

Hugh closed his eyes. "We've all known someone to die, I guess. Aunts. Uncles. Grandparents. But they don't die—" Hugh stopped.

"Because someone wanted them to," Michael finished.

Hugh took a breath. "And it's not like killing a chicken or pig to eat. You take care of them in life. Then you're thankful for the food they give you."

The dead soldier's eyes were glassy and blank. Hugh gently closed them. "I'm not sure why I should be thankful for this man's death."

Ralph's voice made them jump. "Because he was a stinking redcoat."

Ralph's boot came down on the dead soldier's chest. "The British want to walk all over the colonies? Well, it's our turn to walk over them."

Colonial America • 1775

- Massachusetts (Maine)
- New Hampshire
- Massachusetts
- Rhode Island
- Connecticut
- New York
- New Jersey
- Pennsylvania
- Delaware
- Maryland
- Virginia
- North Carolina
- South Carolina
- Georgia

INDIAN RESERVE

SPAIN

British Territory
Spanish Territory
Future State Boundaries

"Show some respect," Hugh said quietly. "The man was doing what he thought was right. Like we are."

Ralph lifted his foot. Then he kicked the dead man's ribs. "That's as much respect as a redcoat deserves," he said. "And if you keep defending the British, I'll report you as a spy."

Hugh's eyes snapped as he rose. Michael stopped him.

"He wants you to fight," Michael hissed.

Hugh watched Ralph go. "I know," he said. He looked down. "But we have work to do."

Hugh turned the body over to take the soldier's coat.

"Looks about my size," Hugh said. He patted the dead soldier's arm. "Thank you."

Hugh and Michael moved to the next body. Then moved to the next.

Finally, Michael packed all the gunpowder packets into one bag. A scream jolted him.

"There's one still alive!" Ralph shrieked. He was racing toward Michael. "I don't have my knife!"

Looking behind Ralph, Michael shrank. Near the trees, a man in a red coat stood.

He was moving closer. His steps were getting faster. He was so close that Michael could see his boots, his buckle, and his face. A face just like—

"Hugh!" Michael shouted.

Hugh crashed to his knees, red coat and all. He couldn't breathe from running and laughing!

By this time, Andrew and Jacob had seen the joke and were laughing too.

Michael couldn't help laughing either.

Ralph had been disrespectful to the dead. And he *had* looked funny, running like a dog.

Christopher didn't laugh. But Michael saw his lips twitch.

Then Michael heard Ralph.

"You'll get yours," Ralph growled.

Chapter 4

Another Enemy

They camped in the woods that night. The main camp was miles behind.

Michael stayed close to Hugh. After all, this was Hugh's first march. When Michael thought about Hugh, he didn't worry about the British or about Ralph.

Michael talked about battles while they put up their tent. "Remember, everyone loads and fires at once," Michael said. "You'll load faster if you rip gunpowder packets with your teeth."

The clothes they slept in were cold as fish scales the next morning. Michael and Hugh huddled in their blankets as

they ate cornmeal mush.

Finally, Hugh stretched. He walked off into the trees.

Michael yawned. He'd go make water too, when Hugh got back.

A shout cut the air. It was the captain. "To arms!"

Michael heard other voices and horse hooves. The British had found them. *The British were here.*

The captain waved the soldiers toward the trees. He pointed to where Hugh had gone!

Michael snatched his gun and Hugh's from the tent. He grabbed bullets and powder.

Michael dashed for the trees. Andrew and Jacob ran behind.

Ralph was already there.

"Where's Hugh?" Michael shouted, getting ready to load.

"Here I am." Hugh took his gun from Michael.

"I thought you'd run off," Ralph grinned. But he looked ready to fight. "After all, you're not much of a man."

Now Michael felt like fighting too. He rammed powder and a bullet down the gun barrel.

"Fire!" the captain shouted. They shot. Then they loaded again.

"Fire!"

Suddenly, British horses and soldiers charged.

Michael gripped both ends of his musket as a shield. A British rider hacked down with his sword. Michael's arms almost snapped.

Then the rider bolted away before Michael could stab him with the gun's bayonet. Michael looked around.

"Hugh!" he shouted.

"He's run off," Ralph barked. "Just like I—"

"Look out!" Michael screamed. The British rider was back. His pistol pointed at Ralph.

A branch dropped. It slapped the redcoat's face. He lurched sideways in the saddle. He tried to shove the branch away.

But it wasn't a branch. It was arms and legs. It was Hugh!

The gun went off. Hugh and the enemy crashed to the earth.

Chapter 5

Soldiers

The redcoat stood. There was no time to think. Michael held up his bayonet. The musket butt punched him as the redcoat ran into the spear.

Michael pulled back as quickly as he could. But the man fell. He landed face down.

Michael didn't want to see his face. But he kept looking down at the man's back.

A bullet snapped into the tree beside him. Suddenly, Michael heard the battle again.

The British soldier lay on the ground beside Hugh. Hugh was trying to move closer to Michael. But his leg wouldn't follow. It was stuck in red mud.

"Grab his arm," Ralph ordered.

Michael obeyed. He didn't want to fight anymore. He bent and shoved his head under Hugh's arm. Ralph did the same.

"This way," Ralph nodded to the right. A field hospital would be set up not far from there.

Panting, the three boys stumbled through the brush. The sounds of the fight grew fainter. Finally, Ralph stopped. He was breathing hard.

They were completely alone in the forest.

"Where is the field hospital?" Michael asked.

"Hospitals are no good if someone wants to live," Ralph said. He bent his knees to lower Hugh to the ground. "Hospitals are full of disease and infection. Soldiers die in there for sure."

Michael knew that was true. But why would Ralph care about Hugh? Ralph hated Hugh. He had sworn to get even.

"You know, Hugh will get in trouble," Michael said. "If he's not in camp. If they can't find his body. They'll say he ran away. The army will discharge him without honor. And no pay."

Hugh was breathing hard. He looked as if he were having a bad dream.

He didn't seem to hear Ralph or Michael.

"Do you really care about Hugh's honor and pay?" Ralph asked. Michael nodded.

"Then we must stay away from the hospital," Ralph said. "We've got to get this bullet out ourselves."

Michael's temper burst. "You've hated Hugh from the start! You said you would get even. How do I know you won't stab him here? Or leave him to die? Why should I trust you?"

"Because Hugh saved my life! Didn't you see that?" Ralph cried. "I'd be dead if not for him. And you might be dead too.

"Hugh deserves a soldier's reward. We won't find that at the hospital. We'd only find disgrace."

"There's no shame in being hurt!" Michael shouted.

"No!" Ralph shouted back. "But something else is wrong with Hugh. The doctor would find out and tell the general. And Hugh would lose everything."

"Ralph is right," said another voice. Hugh looked up at Michael's face.

"What are you talking about?" Michael asked. "You have no disease. No smallpox. There's nothing wrong but a bullet in the leg."

"What's wrong," Hugh looked Michael in the eye, "is that I am a girl."

Chapter 6

One Shot

Michael looked at Ralph. Ralph nodded.

Michael looked back at Hugh. He tried to see a girl's face. He tried to feel the way he felt around girls—careful and unsteady. But all he could see was Hugh.

And Hugh was bleeding badly.

"I don't know what to believe," Michael said. "All I know is we have to do something about this wound. Now."

"I want you to get the bullet out," the wounded soldier said. "Ralph is

right. About everything. And if the doctors find out I'm a girl, the army will lose three soldiers."

"Three?" asked Michael.

"Me, you, and Ralph." She flinched in pain. "Because I'll crown the both of you."

"You and how many of your brothers?" Ralph grinned. He wiped his knife with water from his canteen. Then he held the handkerchief to her mouth. "Here. Bite on this. It's going to hurt more before it hurts less."

Michael had helped kill chickens and pigs before. But that killing was quick. This was pain that lasted. It lasted till they dug out the bullet.

But the hole filled in quickly with blood. The knife was sticky and slippery.

Michael's head was light. He ripped his shirt into bandages. Bloody fingerprints dotted the strips.

Ralph was white. He looked as if his blood had drained too.

Finally, it was over. They passed the water back and forth. The girl closed her eyes.

"How long have you known?" Michael quietly asked Ralph.

"Since just before the attack," Ralph said. "I went to make water. Remember, I walk like an Indian. It's a habit from hunting.

"So she didn't hear me. She was in the woods for the same reason. And . . . well . . ."

"You learned her secret," Michael finished.

Ralph was red. "And you were right about me. I was glad when I found out.

I was going to tell the captain as soon as the battle was over."

"Why didn't you?" Michael asked. He saw the girl's eyes open. But she didn't say anything.

Ralph didn't see her. "I saw the danger we were in. I wanted to help you. But I . . . waited. I waited not to be scared. And Hugh . . . he . . . she was the one who saved us."

Michael was quiet for a while. "War makes a lot of things," he finally said. "But sense isn't one of them."

He looked at the girl.

"So," Michael said. "What's your real name?"

"Kitty," Hugh said. She closed her eyes.

Ralph almost spit the priceless water. "Doesn't sound close to any boy's name I know."

"Where did you get the name 'Hugh'?" Michael asked. "Father? Brother? Dead uncle?"

Kitty smiled weakly. "I wanted to be sure I'd answer when someone called me by a new name. 'Hugh' sounds like 'you.' If someone says, 'Hey, you,' everyone looks. And when I looked, I could see if the speaker meant me."

Michael laughed. Hugh had always been able to make him laugh.

Chapter 7

Steady, Soldier

Michael put one of Kitty's arms over his shoulders. Ralph put the other arm over his. The three limped back to where they had camped last night. It was where they had battled this morning.

"Why were you up in this tree?" Ralph asked as they passed it.

"To see how many were coming," Kitty puffed. "And to take better aim. You learn things like that having brothers."

Michael was not listening. He was looking at the spot where the redcoat had fallen. The body was gone now.

But the tents were still there. And so was the captain.

"Our losses were heavy," the captain said. "I'm glad you weren't among them."

"Sir," Kitty said. "May I leave camp to heal?"

The captain understood. "Rest now. In the morning, you three may go find a nearby home to help you."

Jacob, Andrew, and Christopher moved into another tent. Their new friend would rest better.

Ralph and Michael stayed. But Ralph did not talk with Kitty anymore.

Michael worried. Would Ralph give away her secret after all?

But Michael didn't talk either. Kitty

needed rest. Besides, he felt . . .
careful . . . unsteady around her.

Late that night, Kitty softly called
Michael. He went to see what she
needed.

"We used to talk," Kitty said.

Michael looked at his feet. "I don't
know how to treat you anymore."

"You used to treat me like a friend,"
she said. "What's wrong with that?"

"What's wrong is that nothing makes
sense!" Michael whispered. "I liked
how you were always happy. But you
weren't happy. You don't like being a
girl."

"Yes, I do," Kitty said. "You're the
one who is upset."

"If you were happy, you'd do what
girls do," Michael said. "Girls are so
lucky! They don't have to leave home.
Or take orders from generals. Girls
don't have to hurt. Or kill."

"That's right," Kitty said. "Girls just stay home. They don't take orders from generals. And that's why girls don't become generals.

"Boys are the lucky ones! They can choose. Girls have no choice. Home is a girl's *whole* world."

"Home is my whole world!" Michael said. "Home is why I'm fighting. I'm fighting so my home will be safe. I'm fighting so I can choose laws for my home. I don't want King George choosing for me."

"That's why I'm fighting too!" Kitty said. "I'm fighting for my home. Why is that so hard to understand?"

"Because . . . because girls just don't fight."

Kitty's leg was hurting. Michael could tell. But she smiled at him with half-closed eyes.

"I have nine brothers," Kitty said. "Don't tell *them* girls don't fight."

Chapter

Making Sense of Secrets

In the morning, Michael, Kitty, and Ralph borrowed the captain's horse.

Kitty's leg hurt badly. She couldn't even hold herself up.

Michael and Ralph took turns riding behind her to keep her from falling.

"Where are we going?" Michael asked.

"I came through here on my way to join the army," Ralph said. "I know where there's an inn. Maybe they can take care of her."

"Are you going to tell whoever takes care of you that you're a girl?" Michael asked.

Kitty shook her head. "I want to come back as soon as I'm better. That will be harder to do if townspeople know my secret."

"You don't think anyone will figure it out?" Michael asked.

Kitty tried not to smile. "You didn't," she said.

They arrived at the inn in the late afternoon. Kitty's face drained when they helped her from the horse. Michael knew she hurt.

They ordered supper. They watched the people who worked and ate at the inn. They tried to decide who to ask. Who looked kind enough to care for a hurt soldier?

A woman came to take their empty plates. Ralph paid her and asked for more cider.

"Charge a dollar more!" barked a man nearby. "His money was printed by the colonies. It's worthless! Money printed by King George is worth gold."

Hands on hips, the woman glared at Ralph. "You'd best be leaving. We don't want your kind of money here."

Michael's heart rolled into a ball. He didn't know where else to go. Kitty was tired. Her leg was bleeding a bit through the bandage.

The woman's lips tightened. "I said move along! You're bothering people

who pay *good* money."

Michael and Ralph helped Kitty out. The woman trailed them into the twilight.

"He's hurt," the woman said quietly. "Been fighting the British?"

Ralph slowly nodded.

The woman looked over her shoulder. "Tories come here," she whispered. "Most all the people here are Tories. I hear what they say. I often learn things that help the rebels."

The woman looked Kitty in the eye. "I want to help," she said. "I have a room upstairs. I could take you in the back way. The Tories would never know."

Kitty studied the woman's face. Then she nodded. Kitty turned to Michael and Ralph.

"I will stay here till I heal," she said. "Then I'll come back to the army."

"Are you sure you'll be safe here?" Ralph asked.

Kitty looked at the woman. Their eyes met.

"Yes," Kitty said. "Who knows? I might hear some Tory secrets too."

Michael pressed Kitty's hand. He didn't want to say good-bye. He didn't know if he would ever see Hugh—see her again.

He and Ralph watched the woman help Kitty away. She waved before disappearing around the corner.

Michael stood still. "Nothing makes sense," he said. "A girl pretends to be a boy. A patriot pretends to be a Tory."

Ralph grinned. "The world makes a lot of things. But sense isn't one of them."

Michael looked at Ralph. Slowly, he smiled.

"And for that," he said, "I am glad."

Chapter 9

The Secret Soldier

King George III ruled England in 1782. Kings could tell people where to work and where to go to church.

Many people moved to America to get away from kings and their laws. They wanted to rule themselves. They wanted to make their own laws.

But King George wanted to control the colonies.

The Continental Army was formed to fight King George. The army shocked many people. It was going against the king's law!

Still, the army had no real power. It could not make people join and fight. The army could not even pay its soldiers. Anyone who showed up was welcomed without question.

One of those people was a teacher, Deborah Sampson. In 1782, she dressed as a boy. Then she joined the army in Massachusetts. She called herself "Robert Shurtleff."

Deborah fought bravely in several battles. She hid a bad leg wound. She didn't want doctors to learn her secret.

CANADA

Nova Scotia
Massachusetts (Maine)
New Hampshire
Massachusetts
Rhode Island
Connecticut
New York

But in 1783, Deborah came down with a fever. She was discovered.

General George Washington saw that she got both pay and praise.

But how could it happen? Why didn't the men find out her secret?

- New soldiers did not take fitness tests. They simply signed a piece of paper. And they were in the army!
- Soldiers didn't take many baths. Colonists thought that too many baths were unhealthy! After all, there was no electricity. Army tents were cold. Heating water was hard. Even worse, waters were sometimes polluted. People got sick from bathing in bad water.
- Soldiers slept in their clothes. And like many people, they often had only one set of clothes. Clothes cost a lot.
- Soldiers used camp outhouses. Or they just went into the woods. No one saw.

Soldiers had few reasons to undress in front of one another. Even so, couldn't someone tell a young man from a young woman just by looking?

Maybe they couldn't. Deborah Sampson was taller than most women. She was taller than many men. She tied cloth tightly around her body to make her shape flat. It was like a man's.

Her voice was not as low as many men's. She had no hint of whiskers. But many young men still had high voices and no beards.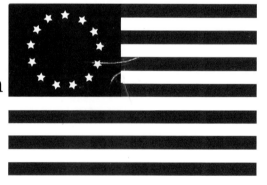

And the army was full of young men. Many lied about their age. They joined before they were 16.

The American Revolution was a war of young people. They fought against worn-out ideas.